Bubba heard a reindeer

eating his kibble

words by Bubba's Dad
illustrated by Faryn Hughes

Illustration by Faryn Hughes
Book design by Kurt Mueller

CreateSpace Independent Publishing Platform,
North Charleston, SC

ISBN-13: 978-1975602550
ISBN-10: 1975602552

Dedication

To my Grandpa,
who loved Christmas.

Bubba

Chapter 1

It was three days after Christmas and Bubba wasn't feeling very well.

He had an upset tummy because he had eaten a gently used Christmas cookie that he found under the sofa.

And he was feeling a little blue because he didn't get everything that was on his Christmas list.

He had asked Santa for two things.
A new monkey toy to play with—
     which he got.
And a new antler to chew on—
     which he didn't.

"What's wrong, Bubba?" asked his new monkey toy. "Don't you want to play?"

"Not really," said Bubba. "I sure wish I had a new antler to chew on."

"Chewing on a new antler always makes me feel better."

"You can chew on my tail if you want," said the new monkey toy trying to be helpful.

"No thank you," sighed Bubba as he put his head on the floor and closed his eyes.

While the new monkey toy sat on top of Bubba's head and played with his big Bubba ears, Bubba tried to think about things other than gently used cookies, and his touchy Frenchie tummy, and not getting everything on his Christmas list.

And that's when he heard it. It was a sound coming from the kitchen upstairs. It was a sound he wasn't expecting. So he listened more carefully.

When the monkey toy pulled on his left ear he listened with his right ear.

"Is that what I think I hear?" he thought to himself.

And when the monkey toy pulled on his right ear he listened with his left ear.

"It sure sounds like what I think I hear," he thought.

Bubba shook his head back and forth, causing his big Bubba ears to flap loudly and sending his new monkey toy flying across the room.

Now with both ears free, Bubba listened, listened very carefully. For the first time in his life he couldn't believe his Bubba ears.

There was someone or something eating his Bubba kibble out of his Bubba bowl.

The monkey toy followed Bubba's gaze up the steps to the kitchen. "Bubba! Who's up there?"

"I don't know, Monkey Toy," Bubba said, "but we're about to find out!"

Chapter 2

Bubba zoomed across the slippery kitchen floor with the monkey toy clutching his collar.

They slid to a stop in front of Bubba's kibble bowl.

"What the monkey?" Bubba exclaimed. "It's empty!"

"Bubba. Who ate your kibble?" shouted the monkey toy.

Bubba sniffed furiously around the bowl with a bunch of loud, snorty Frenchie sniffs.

"I'm not sure. I've never smelled this smell before," said Bubba.

He followed the smell out of the kitchen across the dining room to the sunroom doors.

That's where Bubba stopped. He had to be careful now.

Bubba's mom had a Christmas tree in every room in the Bubba bungalow.

But her biggest and best tree with her most precious ornaments was in the sunroom.

Bubba slowly pushed open the French doors to the sunroom with his short Frenchie nose.

He took a deep breath and peered inside.

"I know you're in there," Bubba said. "Who are you?"

For a moment all was quiet.

And then the big Christmas tree shook ever so slightly.

And Bubba's mom's most precious ornaments tinkled ever so softly.

"Come out. I won't hurt you," Bubba said as calmly as he could.

And that's when something amazing happened.

A soft, velvety nose stuck out from under the tree.

Followed by two big brown eyes.

And two stubby little antlers with more velvet on top.

Bubba's new monkey toy whispered loudly in his big Bubba ear.

"IT'S A BABY REINDEER!"

Chapter 3

Bubba gingerly sniffed the soft velvety nose at his feet.

And the soft velvety nose sniffed back.

"Come out from under there, Baby Reindeer."

"Don't be scared," Bubba
said gently.

The ornaments on the tree tinkled as the baby reindeer wriggled out from under the branches.

He was about the same size as Bubba with a grey coat and a stubby reindeer tail.

"What's your name?"
asked Bubba.

The baby reindeer blinked twice with his big brown eyes but didn't say a word.

"Reindeer can't talk, Bubba," whispered the monkey toy into his ear.

"What do you mean? The reindeer with the red nose on TV talks," said Bubba.

"That's just on TV. That's not real life," said the green polka-dotted monkey toy.

"Oh," said Bubba, looking at the baby reindeer.

"How did you get here? Did Santa bring you?"

The baby reindeer nodded his head up and down.

Bubba thought for a moment.

"Did you hide in his sleigh?"

The baby reindeer nodded his head yes.

"Why did you hide under our tree instead of going home with Santa?"

The reindeer stared at the monkey toy peeking out from behind Bubba's ear.

Bubba looked up over his shoulder at the monkey toy and sighed.

He knew the kind of trouble monkey toys can get you in if you're not careful.

Bubba shook his ears back and forth, sending the monkey toy tumbling to the ground between the reindeer's feet.

"Did you trick the reindeer into staying?" he asked the monkey toy.

"That was naughty."

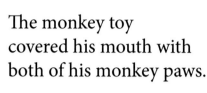

The monkey toy covered his mouth with both of his monkey paws.

"I'm sorry!" the monkey toy blurted out and then covered his mouth again.

Bubba shook his head. "Well, lesson learned I guess."

At that moment Bubba's sensitive Frenchie tummy rumbled.

And the baby reindeer's tummy rumbled, too.

"Are you hungry?" Bubba asked.

The reindeer nodded his head quickly up and down.

"Okay, let's figure out what you like to eat," said Bubba.

"Then we will figure out how to get you back home!"

And with that, Bubba's stubby tail and the reindeer's stubby tail both wagged happily for the first time in three whole days.

Chapter 4

Bubba knew just who to ask what reindeer eat for breakfast.

All he had to do was pull on his winter coat and trudge through the snow across the street to ask his friend Brooklyn Cornelius.

"Cornie" was a super smart French Bulldog who had the answer to everything.

That's because he was a therapy dog who volunteered at the library.

No matter what books kids wanted to read, Cornie would sit with them and they would read them together.

Those kids got super smart that way. And so did Cornie.

"Hi Cornie," said Bubba as his friend came down the front steps to his house.

"Hi Bubba," said Cornie.

Cornie was wearing his red library volunteer bandana, yellow earmuffs and carrying a big green backpack.

"Nice reindeer," said Cornie.

"Thanks," said Bubba.

"You're welcome," said Cornie.

"Do you know what reindeer like to eat?" asked Bubba.

"No, but I can look it up," he said digging through his big green backpack.

When he found the book he was looking for, he sat down and turned a few pages.

His paw skimmed the words and his lips moved while he read.

When he was done reading, he looked up at Bubba and the baby reindeer.

"It says here that reindeer like to eat 'green leafy plants, moss and mushrooms.'"

"Awesome," said Bubba.

"Anything else you need to know?" asked Cornie.

"Just one thing," said Bubba.

"How far is the North Pole from here?"

Cornie dug through his backpack again and pulled out a book filled with maps.

He found the right map and traced a path to the North Pole with his paw.

"Three thousand, one hundred and seventeen miles," said Cornie.

Chapter 5

Bubba trudged through the snow back home.

Then he pulled his green plastic sled out of the snow fort in the front yard.

"We're going to need supplies and a way to carry them," Bubba explained to the baby reindeer.

"We can take turns riding. I will pull first."

So off they went with Bubba pulling the baby reindeer on the sled.

The monkey toy was perched on top of his velvety antlers.

After two blocks they stopped at Oliver's Pizza Place.

"Hi Oliver," Bubba said pushing open the front door.

The delicious smell of pizza filled the air and Bubba licked his short Frenchie nose.

"Hi Bubba," said Oliver, "nice reindeer."

"Thanks," said Bubba, "we need some pizza to go."

"What kind?" asked Oliver.

"Three Green Leafy, Moss & Mushroom pizzas..."

"Two Bubba Kibble pizzas..."

"And one Banana Coconut pizza..."

Bubba's monkey toy tugged on his ear and whispered something.

"With extra bananas," said Bubba.

"Got it," said Oliver.

Then he twirled some pizza dough over his head and tossed it high in the air.

"Bubba, where are you going with all this pizza?" asked Oliver.

"The North Pole," said Bubba.

"Hmm," said Oliver looking at his friend.

"Can I give you some advice, Bubba?"

"Sure," said Bubba.

"Well, you may not know this. But life is like a pizza," smiled Oliver.

"It's more fun when you share. And you have to be careful not to bite off more than you can chew."

Bubba tilted his head and thought about that awhile.

"Hmm, that's good advice. Thanks Oliver."

"You're welcome," said Oliver as he pulled a Green Leafy, Moss & Mushroom pizza out of the oven.

Chapter 6

Bubba and the baby reindeer took turns pulling the sled piled high with pizza boxes.

After what seemed like forever they got to the top of a very steep, very snowy hill.

"Bubba, are we there yet?" asked the monkey toy, tugging on Bubba's ear.

"No, we're not there yet," said Bubba.

"How far do we have to go?" asked the monkey toy.

"Three thousand, one hundred and seventeen miles," said Bubba.

"How far have we gone so far?" asked the monkey toy.

"About six blocks," said Bubba.

Bubba sat on his sled and pondered what to do next.

"This is a really steep hill isn't it, Bubba?" asked the monkey toy.

"Yes it is," said Bubba.

"How are we going to get to the bottom?" said the monkey.

"We are going to pull my sled carefully down the hill so we don't lose our pizza," said Bubba.

The baby reindeer nodded his head in agreement.

"Or we could ride down the hill," the monkey toy suggested cheerfully. "That would be faster and more fun!"

Bubba looked at the pizza boxes and shook his head doubtfully.

"I don't know," said Bubba.

"I think we need to be more careful than that..."

Before Bubba could finish, the monkey toy gave Bubba's sled a little shove and it started sliding down the big hill.

"What could go wrong?" shouted the monkey toy, jumping onto Bubba's head.

As the sled picked up speed, the baby reindeer came bounding down the hill and jumped on board, too.

And that's when they started going really fast...

And the bumps got bigger...

And the ride got scarier...

Bubba steered this way and that as the sled zoomed down the steep hill faster and faster.

Suddenly, Bubba's eyes got very, very big.

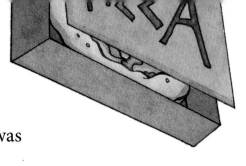

The biggest snow bump
ever appeared and there was
no steering around it.

"Hold on, everybody!" Bubba shouted.

A split second later, Bubba, the baby reindeer,
the monkey toy and three different kinds
of pizza were all tumbling over
and over, high in the bright,
blue winter sky.

Chapter 7

Moe was a very thoughtful pug. And a good neighbor, too.

That's why he was out shoveling the sidewalk for the neighborhood pugs who were too old to do it themselves.

Moe wore a bright blue snowsuit that made him look almost as round as he was tall.

It had little ears on top that stood straight up.

Moe thought his snowsuit ears were funny. And like most pugs, he liked to make people laugh.

So that's why he wore a snowsuit with funny ears.

After shoveling awhile, Moe leaned against his green plastic snow shovel to catch his breath.

When he looked up at the sky, he saw the strangest thing.

A French Bulldog, a baby reindeer, a green polka-dotted monkey and several pizzas went flying over his head.

One by one, they plop, plop, plopped into a big snowbank a little farther down the street.

Moe thought this was a strange development. So he walked down the sidewalk to investigate.

When he got there he found a stubby tail and two velvety antlers sticking out of the snow.

He didn't recognize the antlers, but the stubby tail looked familiar. "Bubba, is that you?" asked Moe.

The stubby tail wagged back and forth.

"Do you need some help?"

The stubby tail wagged a little faster.

"Hold on, Bubba," said Moe as he started shoveling.

Moe was a good snow shoveler, and in a couple of minutes he had Bubba and the baby reindeer dug out of the snow.

"Nice reindeer," said Moe.

"Thanks," said Bubba.

"Where are you taking him?"

"I'm trying to take him back home," said Bubba.

"All the way to the North Pole?" asked Moe.

"Yes, he's lost and he can't get back home without my help," said Bubba.

The baby reindeer blinked and sighed, feeling a little homesick.

"How far is that?" asked Moe.

"Three thousand, one hundred and seventeen miles," said the monkey toy, popping his head out of the snowbank.

"Hmm," thought Moe leaning on his green plastic snow shovel.

"Wouldn't it be easier to send Santa a letter?"

Bubba tilted his head and thought for a moment.

"Brilliant!" said Bubba. "I never thought of that."

"Maybe you could ask Bizzy to help you," said Moe.

"His mom has paper and crayons and envelopes and stamps, too."

"That's another good idea," said Bubba.

And with that, Moe helped Bubba gather up as much gently used pizza as they could find and sent him on his way to find Bizzy.

Chapter 8

Bizzy was a very busy Frenchie.

He was the official greeter at his mom's fabric store, and all day long he raced from the back to the front as customers came and went.

This morning's first customer was an old friend of his.

"Hi Bubba," said Bizzy.

"Hi Bizzy," said Bubba.

"Nice reindeer," said Bizzy.

"Thanks," said Bubba.

"How can I help you?" asked Bizzy the way his mom always did when customers came into the store.

"We were hoping you could help us mail a letter to Santa," said Bubba.

"This baby reindeer is lost and needs to get back home to the North Pole."

"I can help you with that," said Bizzy.

"Shipping and receiving is in the back.
Please follow me."

In the back of the store there was a craft table and many rolls of brightly colored fabric.

Bizzy hopped up on a stool next to the table.

He took a piece of paper and placed it carefully in front of himself.

Then he picked up a big, fat green crayon and held it in his paw.

"Okay," he said. "Let's get started."

Bizzy put the big, fat green crayon against the paper and started writing. He said the words out loud as he wrote them:

> *Deer Santa,*
>
> *Did yew luse a rain deer?*
> *Bubba found him for yew.*
>
> *Sinseerly,*
>
> *Bizzy and Bubba*
>
> *PS: We have bin gud boys this yeer*

Bizzy looked at Bubba and the baby reindeer.

"What do you think?" he asked.

"I think Santa will like that," said Bubba.

The baby reindeer nodded his head up and down. Bubba's monkey toy nodded his head up and down, too.

Bizzy folded the letter and put it in an envelope.

Then he wrote "North Pole" on the front in big green letters.

"I will put two stamps on it, so it gets there extra fast!" said Bizzy.

When he was done, he handed the envelope to Bubba.

"There's a big blue mailbox at the end of the block."

"If you hurry, you can get there before the little white mail truck does."

"Thanks," said Bubba.

"You're welcome," said Bizzy.

"Please come again."

Chapter 9

Bubba held the letter to Santa and looked up at the big blue mailbox.

"What are you thinking, Bubba?" asked the monkey toy.

"I'm thinking I'm too short to put this letter in the mailbox," said Bubba.

"I could climb to the top of the mailbox for you and very carefully put the letter to Santa inside," suggested the monkey toy cheerfully.

Bubba shook his big Bubba ears, sending the monkey flying on top of a snow bank.

"No thank you, Monkey Toy. I learned my lesson," Bubba said.

While Bubba was pondering what to do next, he heard a voice that made his stubby Bubba tail wag super-fast.

"Bubba! Is that you?" the voice called out.

"Mae Ling! Is that you?" Bubba called back.

Bubba couldn't believe his luck.

It was Mae Ling and her sisters Nikko and Lilly, the Frenchie Pile Agility Team!

And they were doing front flips down the sidewalk and headed straight for him.

When they got there, they landed one, two, three... Right on top of each other...

Forming a perfectly balanced tower of Frenchies.

"Oh my dog! Am I happy to see you," said Bubba.

"We have to put this letter to Santa in that little door way up there. Can you help?"

"We sure can," said Mae Ling from the bottom of the Frenchie tower.

"You betcha," said Nikko from the middle.

"Nice reindeer," said Lilly looking down from the top.

"Thank you," said Bubba.

Before he could say anything else, Bubba's very big ears perked up and he listened very carefully.

Off in the distance he could hear the little white mail truck heading in their direction.

"Oh-oh. We have to hurry," said Bubba.

"Don't worry, Bubba. We got this," said Mae Ling.

Then she looked up at her sisters and barked, "Girls, are you ready?"

"Ready!" barked Nikko and Lilly as they somersaulted to the ground.

"Bubba, we're going to need your help, too," said Mae Ling.

"Give the letter to Lilly," she instructed.

"Now stand here in front of the big blue mailbox."

"You're going to be the base and we're going to pile on top. Can you do it?"

"I think so," said Bubba.

"Okay, team. Let's go!" Mae Ling barked.

What happened next was pretty amazing.

Mae Ling did a back flip and landed firmly on top of Bubba...

Nikko did two front flips and landed smack dab on top of Mae Ling...

Then Lilly did three cartwheels and blasted off high into the air...

When she came down she made a perfect four-paw landing on top of the world's tallest tower of Frenchies!

And that's when a little problem arose...

Mae Ling felt the Frenchie tower start to sway.

A little to the right. And a little to the left.

"Are you doing okay, Bubba?" she asked.

"I think so," said Bubba, his knees feeling a little wobbly.

"Lilly, how about you! Can you reach?"

Lilly stretched and stretched as far as her Frenchie paw would stretch and...

"I can't quite reach!" said Lilly. "I need some help!"

Bubba could feel his Bubba knees getting wobblier and wobblier.

And his Bubba ears could hear the little white mail truck getting closer and closer.

He knew that time was running out.

And he knew what he had to do.

He had to convince the monkey toy not to be naughty. Just this once.

"Monkey Toy," Bubba said kindly but firmly. "We need your help."

The monkey toy pointed at himself, surprised that Bubba was talking to him.

"Me?" said the monkey toy, his eyes as big as his polka dots.

"Yes, you, Monkey Toy. You can do it," said Bubba.

The monkey toy looked into Bubba's eyes.

"You trust me?" asked the monkey toy.

Bubba looked into the monkey toy's eyes.

"Yes, I trust you," said Bubba.

And that's when something truly amazing happened.

For the first time in his life, the monkey toy didn't feel naughty. He felt like he could be trusted.

And it felt good.

"Okay, Bubba," said the monkey toy. "I will try."

"Good," said Bubba. "You and the baby reindeer can do it together."

That's all the monkey toy needed to hear.

In a flash, he grabbed the baby reindeer's stubby tail and swung himself up onto his velvety antlers.

Without missing a beat, the baby reindeer gave his antlers a quick flip.

And the monkey toy went flying high to the top of the big blue mailbox.

From there the monkey toy pushed open the little door with his paws.

Then Lilly stretched and stretched just far enough to drop the envelope inside.

And at that moment...Bubba's wobbly knees gave out completely!

And he and Mae Ling and Nikko and Lilly collapsed into a giggling pile of Frenchies...

Just as the little white mail truck came sliding to a stop next to the big blue mailbox.

Chapter 10

For the next two sleeps Bubba and the baby reindeer and the monkey toy waited.

And waited. And waited.

Each morning they would wake up hoping Santa had come the night before.

But he didn't come. Not yet anyway.

Luckily, Bubba was an unusually optimistic Frenchie. He knew that Santa was coming.

It was only a matter of time.

So he used the time he and the baby reindeer had together to become really good friends.

Each morning the baby reindeer would eat his gently used Green Leafy, Moss & Mushroom pizza out of Bubba's bowl.

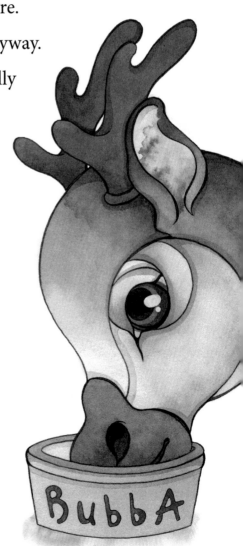

Then Bubba would eat his special Bubba kibble
for sensitive Frenchie tummies.

After that they would go outside and play in Bubba's
snow fort and chase each other around the frozen
fountain in the backyard.

And each night Bubba would tuck his monkey toy
into the toy box where his monkey toys slept.

Then Bubba and the baby reindeer would snuggle
into Bubba's fleecy cave bed…

And quickly fall asleep.

But even while they slept, Bubba's ears would stay wide awake.

Listening, listening very carefully.

Then late on the third night he heard it.

The baby reindeer didn't hear it. The monkey toy didn't hear it. But Bubba's very big ears heard it quite clearly.

It was Santa's sleigh. And it was headed this way!

Bubba opened his eyes and looked over at the baby reindeer sleeping next to him.

A few seconds later, Santa's sleigh slid to a stop on top of the bungalow.

Bubba gently nudged his new friend with his short Frenchie nose.

"Wake up, he's here," said Bubba softly.

The baby reindeer's eyes popped wide open.

They got even wider when he heard the grown-up reindeer on the roof jingle their bells.

The sound made him wag his stubby reindeer tail. But then it stopped wagging.

He looked over at Bubba, blinked twice and made a soft baby reindeer sigh. He sure was going to miss his new friend.

Bubba sighed a big Bubba sigh. He felt the same way.

"Goodbye, Baby Reindeer. I sure am going to miss you," Bubba said.

The grown-up reindeer on the roof jingled their bells a little louder. And the baby reindeer knew it was time to go.

So he nuzzled Bubba with his soft velvety nose...

And Bubba nuzzled him back...

Then the baby reindeer slipped out of the fleecy cave bed...

Ran up the stairs and out Bubba's doggy door...

Right into Santa's waiting arms.

###

Now the Bubba bungalow was quiet again.

The monkey toy hopped into the fleecy cave bed next to Bubba so he wouldn't be lonely.

And Bubba started to drift off to sleep.

For a moment he thought he could hear the baby reindeer's little hooves dancing around the big Christmas tree upstairs.

And that made his stubby Bubba tail wag.

But Bubba knew that was probably just a dream.

A wonderful, happy dream.

So he wagged his stubby Bubba tail a few more times. Then drifted off to a very deep and very happy sleep.

Chapter 10 ½

The next morning Bubba woke up to his mom calling his name.

"Bubba!" she called from the sunroom.

"Come quick. You have a present!"

Bubba flew out of his fleecy cave bed like he was shot out of a cannon.

He was up the stairs and sliding to a stop in front of the big Christmas tree in two seconds flat.

"I don't know how we missed it the first time," Bubba's mom said, shaking her head.

And that's when Bubba saw it.

A brand new antler. Wrapped in a big green bow. The best Christmas present ever!

That is all.

Follow Bubba on Facebook

Keep up with Bubba's real-life
and storybook adventures on Facebook
@ Bubba Louie Book Page

About Bubba

The real Bubba is a French Bulldog
and virtual Assistant Mascot at the Muleshoe
Area Public Library. In addition to being
an author, he is also a Certified Therapy Dog
who goes on hospice visits with his dad
and school visits with his mom.

Bubba's Dad

is a writer of children's books and many
other things with words in them. He lives
with Bubba and Bubba's mom in Minnesota
and in California sometimes, too.
He has his own name but most people
just call him Bubba's Dad.

Faryn Hughes

is an illustrator of utopian
and whimsical water-medium works,
imaginative storybook designs for children,
and folklore inspired scenes.
She is also a cat mom to Cash and Finnegan,
who she adores.

Come to the Rescue

Please give generously
to your favorite animal rescue organization.
Two of Bubba's favorites are:

French Bulldog Rescue Network
www.frenchbulldogrescue.org

S.N.O.R.T.
Short Noses Only Rescue Team
www.snortrescue.org

Did you like my book?

If you enjoyed my book,
leave a good review on Amazon.

I can't wait to read
your comments!

Bubba

Made in the USA
Lexington, KY
03 October 2018